D1052535

Dear Parent:
Your child's love of reading starts here!

Every child learns to read in a different way and at his or her own speed. Some go back and forth between reading levels and read favorite books again and again. Others read through each level in order. You can help your young reader improve and become more confident by encouraging his or her own interests and abilities. From books your child reads with you to the first books he or she reads alone, there are I Can Read Books for every stage of reading:

SHARED READING
Basic language, word repetition, and whimsical illustrations, ideal for sharing with your emergent reader

BEGINNING READING
Short sentences, familiar words, and simple concepts for children eager to read on their own

READING WITH HELP
Engaging stories, longer sentences, and language play for developing readers

READING ALONE
Complex plots, challenging vocabulary, and high-interest topics for the independent reader

ADVANCED READING
Short paragraphs, chapters, and exciting themes for the perfect bridge to chapter books

I Can Read Books have introduced children to the joy of reading since 1957. Featuring award-winning authors and illustrators and a fabulous cast of beloved characters, I Can Read Books set the standard for beginning readers.

A lifetime of discovery begins with the magical words "I Can Read!"

Visit www.icanread.com for information
on enriching your child's reading experience.

I Can Read Book® is a trademark of HarperCollins Publishers.

Transformers: Hunt for the Decepticons: Buddy Brawl
HASBRO and its logo, TRANSFORMERS and all related characters are trademarks of Hasbro and are used with permission. © 2010
Hasbro. All Rights Reserved. Manufactured in China.
No part of this book may be used or reproduced in any manner whatsoever without written permission except in the case of
brief quotations embodied in critical articles and reviews. For information address HarperCollins Children's Books, a division of
HarperCollins Publishers, 10 East 53rd Street, New York, NY 10022.
www.icanread.com

Library of Congress catalog card number: 2010922251
ISBN 978-0-06-199176-9
Typography by John Sazaklis

10 11 12 13 14 SCP 10 9 8 7 6 5 4 3 2 1   ❖   First Edition

I Can Read!

READING 2 WITH HELP

TRANSFORMERS

Buddy Brawl

HUNT for the DECEPTICONS
TRANSFORMERS.com

Adapted by Lucy Rosen

Illustrations by MADA Design, Inc.

HARPER

An Imprint of HarperCollins*Publishers*

Bumblebee and Wheelie

are two clever Autobots.

They are always ready

to fight the Decepticons.

One day, Sam and Mikaela
were driving through the city
with Wheelie and Bumblebee.

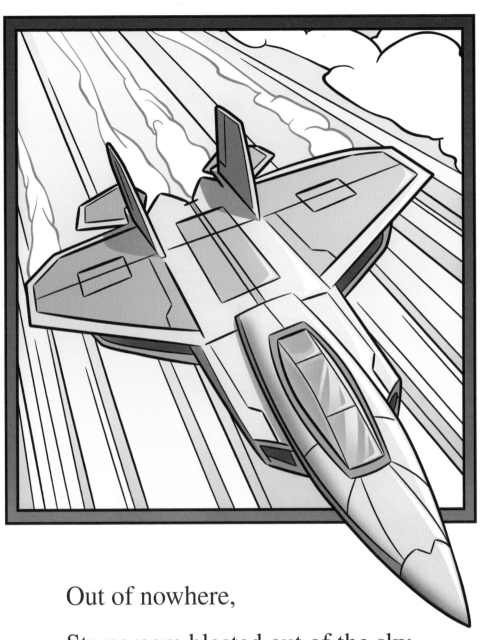

Out of nowhere,

Starscream blasted out of the sky

and swooped in to attack!

Wheelie and Bumblebee

had to protect Sam and Mikaela.

"Starscream is smart," said Wheelie.

"We have to trick, trick, trick him!"

"No," said Bumblebee

through his car radio.

"Starscream can't fly without his wings.

We must destroy them!"

"That idea is bad, bad, bad!"

said Wheelie.

"Your plan won't work!"

said Bumblebee.

"Guys," yelled Sam and Mikaela.

"We could use a little help here!

Stop fighting each other and start

fighting this Decepticon!"

But Bumblebee and Wheelie

weren't paying attention.

They were too busy yelling.

With one powerful punch,

he hit Starscream

and knocked him out cold.

"That was a close call,"
Optimus told Wheelie
and Bumblebee.
"You two hotheaded robots
better learn to work together.
I may not be around
the next time a Decepticon
tries to attack our friends."

Wheelie and Bumblebee

knew that Optimus was right.

But that didn't mean their fight was over.

Bumblebee and Wheelie

would not speak to each other!

Sam and Mikaela tried to get

their friends to talk.

"Tell Wheelie that you're sorry,"
Sam told Bumblebee.
But Bumblebee changed into
a car and sped away.

"Come on," Mikaela said to Wheelie.

"Can't you two make up?"

"No, no, no!" said Wheelie.

"Never, never, never!"

Even Optimus Prime
couldn't end the fight.
"Give them time," he said.
"They'll have to learn that
Autobots always stick together."

But Bumblebee and Wheelie

were out of time.

Starscream was ready

to attack again.

"I'll get you this time!" he yelled.

"I'll save Sam and Mikaela,"

said Optimus.

"You two, stop Starscream!"

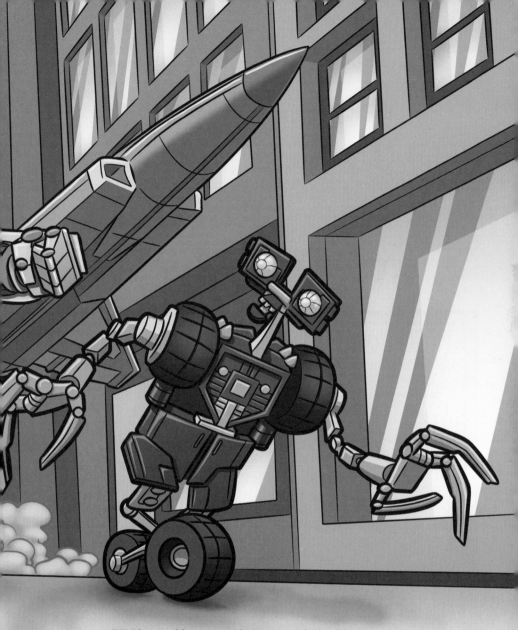

Wheelie and Bumblebee

looked at each other.

They had to act fast.

"Follow me, Decepticon!"

said Wheelie.

He zigged and zagged

through the city streets.

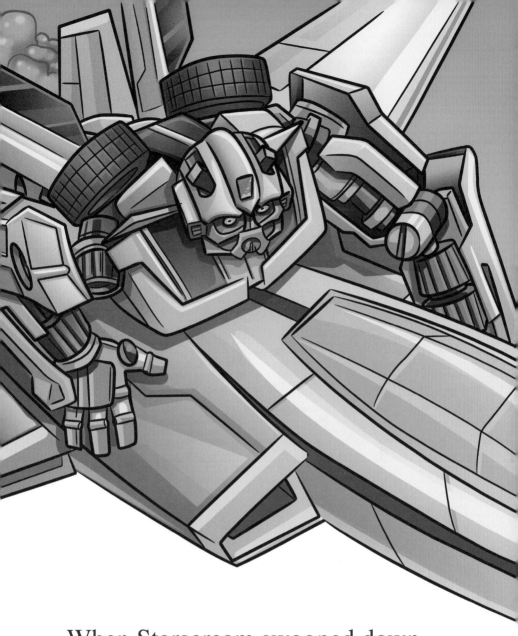

When Starscream swooped down
to try and catch Wheelie,
Bumblebee jumped on his back!

Wheelie was about to reach a tunnel.

Bumblebee steered Starscream

right into the tunnel's opening.

CRASH!

Starscream couldn't fit through the tunnel.

His wings crumpled.

"We did it!

We did it together!"

said Wheelie and Bumblee.

They gave each other a high five.

"Thanks for tricking Starscream

into that tunnel,"

said Bumblebee.

"Thanks, thanks, thanks

for helping!"

said Wheelie.

"Optimus was right," said Bumblebee.
"Two Autobots are always
better than one!"